NIGHTMARE

Order this book online at www.trafford.com
or email orders@trafford.com

Most Trafford titles are also available at major online book retailers.

Printed in the United States of America.

ISBN: 978-1-4269-4837-4 (sc)
ISBN: 978-1-4269-4959-3 (e)

Trafford rev. 11/20/2010

 www.trafford.com

North America & international
toll-free: 1 888 232 4444 (USA & Canada)
phone: 250 383 6864 ♦ fax: 812 355 4082

NIGHTMARE

Zander Griffyn

CONTENTS

PROLOGUE

October 8, 2001

Yesterday at school my English teacher gave an assignment for us to write in our journals about what's on our minds. I thought it was worthless, so I decided not to do it. Of course, I got in trouble for not doing it, but I just can't write all that's on my mind. There is just too much.

October 10, 2001

This afternoon I attempted to write it all down. I found out I wasn't being sent to the principal's office; I was being sent to Mrs. Miller, the school's psychologist. She has been in the school since the incident. All the kids are talking about her. Some say she's good, others say she's being nosy. I don't know what to make of her except that she, too, wants me to write my thoughts. And well, my thoughts just seem to ramble endlessly.

October 15, 2001

Last night I woke up with beads of sweat on my forehead and heard some noises. I didn't really get up 'cause all I did was hide under the covers. The president interrupted the TV show that was airing to announce that we had gone down to a Yellow Alert, but I just don't believe him. What if they come back? What if they try it again? I haven't been able to concentrate in school. I got my first D in Spanish yesterday. Mrs. Alvarez pulled me aside at the end of the period and asked if everything was okay. I began to tell her about my dreams, but all that came out was, "I think I had a nightmare, and it kept me up all night." Then the bell rang and more kids started coming in. She smiled sheepishly and told me to make an appointment with Mrs. Miller.

October 17, 2001

So I saw Mrs. Miller this afternoon. I sat in her office eating chocolate chip cookies. She asked me about the recent D I got in Spanish. I told her I hadn't studied, but that was a lie, and I didn't want to lie to her. So then I told her about my nightmares. I told her that I kept having the same nightmare over and over again every night. In this nightmare I see my friends and family members falling from the two buildings. I try to wake up, but I just can't. It is as though I have to watch the whole nightmare. It's totally dreadful.

It was hard for me to tell Mrs. Miller without tearing up and acting unmanly. I felt like a baby again, being scared of nightmares and just wanting to run to my mom. She wrapped her arms around me in attempt to comfort me, but I broke away, tears rushing down my cheeks. My mind now endlessly played the nightmare over and over again, and I didn't care if Mrs. Miller was trying to placate me.

February 11, 2002

I am still having the horrid nightmare three times a week. I always wake up with my hands trembling and sweat dripping from my brow. I don't know why. It is just randomly happening.

Mrs. Miller says we are making progress. In today's session, I finally told her what actually happened on that day. Our science teacher, Mr. Grossman, had organized a field trip for the sixth-grade Science Discovery Club. We were headed to visit the Liberty Science Museum in New Jersey. It was 9 a.m., and the second bus had just left Battery Park City Middle School, but my bus had had already made its way past the Lincoln Tunnel into New Jersey. The few moments after that are what keep replaying in my head over and over again.

The driver had parked the bus along the road and had summoned Mr. Grossman to the front to speak to him in private. He had a small, gray, pocket-sized radio in his hand, and he was waving his hand in front of us, telling us to be quiet. I stared intently at their mouths, trying to read their lips and make sense of what they were saying. The driver seemed extremely anxious. All I heard was Mr. Grossman yell, "Slow down and take a deep breath," when I looked out the right side of the bus and into the side-view mirror and suddenly saw a big cloud of gray ash engulf Manhattan.

The entire bus had hushed when a sudden tremor rocked it moments later. You could hear the silence and see the deadly terror in both Mr. Grossman and the driver's faces. We were immediately told to duck under our seats. I remember looking out at one point with the camera I had taken with me, and I focused in on the blazing building only to see tiny specks jumping out. I didn't know it then, but those were actual people jumping out, escaping the flames that engulfed the tower of terror.

That is what haunts me at night now. But in my nightmares, it's my mom and dad, my brother and my friends falling down. But it doesn't end there. Several school days after the field trip, I realized my friend Kris hadn't been to school ever since the tragedy. I was very curious about his absence, for he was a very good friend of mine. We always played manhunt and wall ball at recess. We always went to each other's houses to play video games. Kris would come swim in my family's pool on the scorching days of summer, and we would have a blast. He was a year older than me and in the seventh grade, but age was no factor for us.

A week after the incident, the principal of the school announced over the loud speaker, "Students and teachers, please report to the gymnasium for an emergency assembly." The class quickly gathered into a single-file line. We walked out of the classroom and into the hallway to meet up with the other sixth-grade classes. We continued down the corridor to the two big doors of the gymnasium. You could hear the kids' murmurs as they tried to figure out what was going on. We all took our places on the slick hardwood of the gym. As I sat down, I saw Mrs. Teague crying behind the stage curtains and several others with tissue boxes in their hands. The principal was there, along with the vice principal and a couple of people dressed in formal outfits. They looked important.

The whole school was seated on the floor, hardly any space to move around. A policeman came up to the podium with a sheet of paper in his hands. What was this all about? I thought. This must be very important for a policeman to be involved. The principal greeted the policeman and shuffled to the left of the small, brown podium, which featured the logo of the Battery Park City Gladiators. The policeman signaled the gym to hush, and full silence fell. He cleared his throat and spoke aloud in a quivering voice, "Students and teachers of Battery Park City Middle School, I have dire and heartbreaking news. Kris Wahl of Mrs. Teague's seventh-grade class was killed in the collapse of the Twin Towers." The many gasps orchestrated from the gymnasium like a church choir. "Kris was an obedient student who always strove toward success. He ..."

My mind became numb. It blocked out the rest of the policeman's words. I didn't move. I was frozen. How could this have happened? Mr. Grossman awoke me from my sudden swoon. I felt two streams of dampness on my cheeks. I must've been crying. Mr. Grossman must have seen and come to comfort me. He asked me if I was feeling okay, but I couldn't reply. Tears rushed out in a flash flood.

February 26, 2002

Yesterday my parents had a small surprise birthday party for me. I turned twelve. So what's so amazing about twelve?

I still can't sleep at night. I often wake up with dark circles under my eyes. I'm failing Spanish and Science. And Mrs. Miller said I have post-traumatic stress disorder—PTSD. It's something that happens to people who have experienced a very traumatic event. I think I'm losing my mind. I hardly go out anymore, afraid that I will be away from my parents, just like on that day. Craig and Leah were here yesterday, but our friendship has not been the same. They say I don't laugh anymore; they say I've lost my sense of humor. But I say, what's there to laugh about? We just made small talk. Most of what was on our minds was talk about the incident. That's what we call it now—the incident. Most of the adults sat around and just talked about where they were when it happened. I don't think anyone was as close to it as I was.

Sometimes I hear Mom and Dad talking through the vents at night, and they're scared too. Last night they were talking about making emergency plans in case something else happened. I'm really scared, and I think Craig and Leah are too. We made a pact yesterday to always stick together. No matter what.

June 24, 2002

Well, I got my report card today. And I saw Mrs. Miller for our last session. She says I am progressing well. She spent some time talking to my mom and Mr. Grossman outside her office. I was able to take a peek at her notes. The evaluation said, "Continues with preoccupation of traumatic event, needs continual intervention … will continue to see him through summer." On the corner of the page she'd scribbled, "Quiet lamb … needs shepherd."

She ended our session with a hug and a smile and said she would see me again in two weeks. There goes my summer … but what else am I going to do, anyway? Mom and Dad have not scheduled our usual summer vacation to the Adirondacks. Last week they cancelled our trip to the city to see the circus. And even now, my head is still buzzing about the scribble on the corner of Mrs. Miller's evaluation.

January 2, 2003

Yesterday was New Year's Day. My resolution was to not be scared or ignorant of that knocking I always hear at night. I want to be able to figure out what that noise is. But could it be my mind playing tricks on me? Or is it more than—

1

THE CLAMOR AT NIGHT

It was a cold, thundery night in a Battery Park City apartment. Max opened his closet and grabbed his bathrobe. He put it on for warmth, for it was certainly below thirty degrees, and continued doing his homework. The thunder roared, and the lightning flashed. The thunder sounded more like cracks of a whip than rumbles. The flashes of lightning beamed through Max's bedroom window.

On his seventh math problem, the lights dimmed and then went out. Silence. Max didn't move a muscle. He stayed in his seat until his mother came with candles. Max knew the candles were apple pie scented, his mother's favorite. He smelled them as she walked in.

"Are you okay, Max?" his mother asked as she placed one candle on his night table.

"Yes, I'm fine. I just didn't finish my math homework," he said, closing his thick, heavy textbook and slipping a pocket-sized journal inside it. He stared at the glowing glare of the candle on his night table.

"I brought this candle for you to find your way around," his mother said. "Don't worry about your homework. You can finish it in the morning when the storm's over. I'll go check on Tommy." She gave Max a kiss on the forehead. "Don't stay up too late," she added.

Max loved being kissed by his mother. Whenever she kissed him, he felt secure. These kisses showed his mother's affection for him, and he always returned them with a radiant smile. It was comforting to know his mother would always be there to guide him in the right direction and to hold him when he was terrified.

After a few minutes, Max's father entered his room quietly. He knelt by the side of his bed and said, "Good night, Max, good night." He ruffled the boy's hair and patted his back.

"Good night, Dad," said Max, getting snug under his wool quilt. The wool quilt prickled his skin and made him want to scratch, but he didn't want to leave the coziness of his covers. After a while, Max fell into a deep sleep.

"If we cannot stop this, what else can we not stop?"

Max awoke to the sound of his own voice. And the other noise. *Plethunk!* He was lethargic yet full of energy at hearing the noise once more while awake. He checked his alarm clock. 1:13. He heard it again—*Plethunk!* That noise, that clamor, where was it coming from? Max thought of the last two years and the noise he had heard so often. He used to be afraid of the noise, but soon he adapted to the clamorous nights and ignored it. But now he would hold to the resolution he had made the day before and check out what was making the nightly din.

Max crept out of his bed and treaded softly toward his parents' room. The floor creaked beneath his every step. He twisted the doorknob, gently pushed the door, and peeked in. They were sound asleep. He inched in and looked behind the door, but he saw nothing but his mom's bathrobe dangling from a hook. It almost looked like a body, but he blinked to take a second glance and then closed the door.

Max crept down to the kitchen and flicked the light on. The side door leading to the backyard was closed, and so was the kitchen window. Nothing. He tiptoed back up to his brother's room. *Maybe Tommy had gone to the bathroom*, he thought. But Tommy was sound asleep, snoring the way he always did.

Max never knew why he, his brother, and his father snored. His shoulders jiggled up and down as he entertained the thought that this could easily be the loud clamor he had heard. But at that moment Max heard it again, and it stopped him dead in his tracks. He stared a little more intently around at his surroundings. He looked at the clock on the wall and all the toys on the floor. In the dark silence of the night, the toys seemed like menacing ghouls staring back at him. He rubbed his eyes to clear his vision and then eventually gave up his search.

Max went back to his bedroom, forgetting about the noise, the clamor that had stirred him from his sleep. He decided that it was his mind playing tricks on him. He climbed back into bed and lay in silence for a few more minutes, his eyes becoming heavy from lack of sleep.

Plethunk! Max heard it again. This time he knew where it was coming from. He pulled the wool quilt off of his body and stood up, dreadfully tired but also dreadfully scared. He looked for something he could use as a weapon but found nothing but a deck of cards that had spilled onto the floor when he'd first sat up earlier. Max could feel fear slithering up his spine. He bent down and looked under his bed. Nothing. His whole body shivered as he nervously stood up and walked to his closet. He reached for the doorknob and then hesitated. He felt dread slide down his arms as the hairs on the back of his neck stood up and he froze in his stance. He grasped the doorknob, questioning what might lie behind the door.

Perspiration trickled down his face as he twisted the knob. He pulled on the door and was frightened out of his mind at what he saw. The clamor that had kept him up all night the last two years—the thing in his closet was … *a horse*! It neighed and exhaled smoke from its nostrils. It thumped its hooves on the carpeted floor. Wings of fire appeared out of the horse's chestnut sides as it stepped out of the closet, glowing brightly in the middle of Max's bedroom. Max stumbled backward, jaw dropped and his eyes staring in bewilderment.

"I am Elzara, a Nightmare," the horse spoke. Max noticed the horse had a tail that flared with flames. It singed the wall and left behind a black, ash-burnt spot.

"What do you mean Nightmare?" Max asked incredulously.

Elzara trotted forward, forcing Max to move farther back. "I am a mare, a female horse, and I come at night," Elzara replied. "I am a Nightmare. I am your sentinel, and I have been called to guard you, Max Weston."

"From what are you guarding me, and how do you know my name?" asked Max.

"I am guarding you from the Shadowa, an evil faction of shadowed creatures trying to eliminate mankind and make Earth their realm. And I, a Nightmare, your guardian, have been summoned from the world of dreams to keep you from falling into their snare."

"Elzara, why am I in danger?" Max inquired.

A spurt of fire shot out of Elzara's nostrils as she trotted around the room. Her wings, mane, and tail displayed a fiery glow that filled the room with an abundance of light. Quickly she answered, "To the Shadowa, you and your family are weak, Max. They have been observing you for quite some time. You live a mind-numbing, wearisome life. You wake up, eat breakfast, go to school, learn what is not interesting to you, then come home again, eat some more, and go to sleep. And you start all over again the next day. Tell me, Max, when was the last time you looked up at the stars? Or made a friend? Or gave it your all during the baseball game? Why have you stopped trying? To the Shadowa, you are a Dark Soul because you do not attempt anything anymore. Life is meaningless to you. You have been filled with fear and hopelessness. On my planet you would be referred to as a lily-livered lad. The Shadowa love those who take each day for granted and are fear-filled and hate those who try new things. You've given up! They want your soul, Max."

Max's nostrils flared in fear and disbelief as he stated incredulously, "I never looked at it that way … am I really that uninteresting? Have I really given up?" Scenes of Max's life flashed before his eyes, and he raised an eyebrow. "I can't remember the last time I made a friend. Craig has been my friend since kindergarten, and Leah since second grade." Max paused, for the next name to be said would be Kris's.

Max's mind stopped, flashing on one particular scene in his life, when he was eleven years old two years ago. He was walking to school, his shoulders hunched over by the weight of his heavy backpack. The Max in the reminiscence just walked, but Max in the present could see vague shadows crawling behind the alias-Max.

"On this planet of yours, there are many Dark Souls roaming around, living life in a monotonous fashion. But you, Max, are different. You've fallen into a lull, and I am here to awaken you to the possibilities. You are young; you are the next generation, and you can lead your family and this whole Earth to the path that has been predestined for you."

Max suddenly felt a huge burden. He felt like Atlas, the Greek god he had been studying in history class at school, who carried the world on his shoulders. But somehow he understood what he was being called to do. He wanted to protect his family and his little brother, Tommy, most of all. Tommy looked up to him. But most days, Max just gave him the cold shoulder and shooed him to another room or locked himself in his own room while he played the latest popular video game, called *Zombified*. But ever since he lost his friend Kris he has felt a tighter bond to Tommy.

All of a sudden, there was a thunderous bellow. It shook the whole house. Max was frightened as he tried to maintain his balance.

"Elzara, what was that, that rumbling noise?" he asked, his voice trembling in fear.

"It is the roar of the trumpet of the Shadowa. They blast it when they have taken over a Dark Soul. It is a very tragic moment for us Nightmares. That Nightmare lost the battle, and we have lost another young human to the other side. The Shadowan has eliminated its prey and sucked its soul."

"Is that what can happen to me if I continue to live life the way I have?" Max asked, already knowing the response Elzara would give him.

"Desolately, yes."

"Have you seen or encountered a Shadowan?"

"Yes, and it was not a pretty sight," Elzara said, staring languorously at the ceiling. "It wore a black and red gown with a hood that covered its face entirely, only leaving unveiled its yellow eyes. It had horribly lengthy nails about four to six inches long and translucent, black wings made of a thin membrane that cannot be seen at night, making it look as though it were floating."

"Are there any male night horses, stallions?" Max asked, changing the subject.

"No. Only females live on our star, Trepiti," the mare answered as she trotted back and forth in the bedroom. Max was now lying in his bed, listening to his guardian and pondering on her every word.

"I have been waiting, Max," she continued. "Not just for you to find me, the cause of the clamor, but for you to take a stand and not be afraid. For two years I've been waiting for you."

Max glanced at his alarm clock. 1:59. There was silence for a few seconds. He heard light thumps coming from the long, narrow hallway outside his bedroom. He knew it was his mother. She was a light sleeper, after all. She could hear you whisper in your sleep.

"Go back to where you came from, Elzara; my mother is coming. If she sees you, she'll freak out," Max whispered briskly. He quickly pulled the wool quilt cover over himself as Elzara trotted softly back into his closet.

Max's mother opened the door and held an apple-pie-scented candle in her hand. Max pretended he was asleep. His heart beat furiously. He tried to calm his thoughts and forget that he had just been talking to his "Nightmare." His mother smiled as she looked down at Max. She strode back to the door and closed it behind her. The radiant glow of the candle vanished from Max's room, and darkness took over.

2

A CLOSE ENCOUNTER

Max awoke to his alarm clock. 6:30 a.m. He slammed the snooze button and stayed lying in his bed. He gazed at the closet, wondering if the events of last night really took place. Looking at the wall, he saw no singe marks. But when he gave the wall a second glance, he could've sworn he saw a burnt spot. He sat up on his elbows to get a better look, and there it was—a black, ash-burnt spot. He fell back onto the bed and stared at the ceiling. This time he was really frightened.

Why was he a Dark Soul? How could he change? How could he save his family and the world? He wanted to see Elzara again. He wanted to make sure he hadn't been dreaming. He squeezed his eyes shut and hoped to see a Nightmare, but it was daylight, and he realized his Nightmare would not come.

Being a target for a Shadowan, of course, gave Max an uneasy feeling. It made him afraid, aware of his every move. It felt like there was someone watching him. It was as though someone was waiting for him to fail, complain, give up, and surrender his future.

Max yanked the wool quilt off and eased his feet into his blue slippers. He treaded to the bathroom sluggishly, not only from drowsiness, but from the immense news he'd taken on late last night. He brushed his teeth. After that, he dressed in his school clothes and threw his pajamas into the hamper. Max fixed his bed and darted to the kitchen.

His mother and father sat at the kitchen counter, sipping their coffee quietly. Mrs. Weston took a bite of her jellied toast and said, "Good morning. What shall I make for you?"

"Good morning, Mom and Dad. I'm really in the mood for pancakes. How 'bout *chocolate* pancakes?" Max replied, grasping the remote for the TV. When he was a child, chocolate pancakes had always made him feel happy and lighthearted. Maybe Max could achieve joy with chocolate pancakes.

He pushed the on button, and full-color images appeared on the screen. He changed the channel to cartoons and placed the remote beside him.

Max heard his mother stirring the pancake batter and then pouring it onto the electric griddle. He whiffed the sweet aroma of the pancakes and the Hershey's chocolate. The addicting smell made Max want to ask if the pancakes were ready, but he knew they weren't, so he just waited.

Soon enough, Max was sitting at the table with his chocolate pancakes soaked with maple syrup. Max always drowned his pancakes with syrup. It was so sweet and delectable. He sat at the table enjoying his pancakes and enjoying watching his mom and dad. *Life is as sweet as pancakes*, thought Max, optimistically. *It would be much sweeter if I knew there weren't any shadowed creatures interested in my soul.*

After breakfast, Max made his way to the bus stop where his friends Craig and Leah were waiting for him. They did their secret handshake—pound, clap, back clap, and another pound. All three had met in the early years of elementary school. Craig was twelve years old, and Leah was ten. The age difference didn't matter to them; all they knew was that they got along well.

Max glanced out the window as the bus stopped again. Two boys boarded the bus. Max saw a shadow and traced it. It was not of the bus, the trees, or the stop sign, but of a tall, slender figure similar to a human being. The bus moved on slowly, and the shadow stayed in its place. He was perplexed. Maybe something was wrong with his vision. He rubbed his eyes.

Then, as if out of a sci-fi movie, the dark shadow sprouted wings out of its back and then disappeared. Max was confused and scared. Was he dreaming or being followed? He couldn't quite make it out. He felt as though he'd been catapulted into a pool of fear and confusion.

The bus eased to the curb of the school, and children poured out like sand out of a pail. The motion of all the students was like a strong tide dragging Max to the steps of the school.

Now everywhere he looked, he saw shadows. They were behind trees and cars. He saw shadows following some of the kids. He saw the shadows enter the giant, brick school.

The school day dragged on, and Max could not concentrate on his work. He stared out the windows of his every class while his fellow students were engaged in their work. All he wanted was to see Elzara and to put his mind at ease.

Arriving home that afternoon, Max's mother greeted him as he opened the front door. She gave him a big hug, noticing the rings under his eyes. She had become accustomed to them since the dreadful event. "Rough day, huh, Max?" she said, giving him a kiss on the forehead. "Don't forget we've got swimming lessons today at four thirty, so complete your homework before then. Your brother will be here soon," Mrs. Weston added as she made her way into the kitchen.

Max ran to his room, threw his backpack on the floor, and reclined on his bed. Yes, this was comfortable. He could finally relax. He dozed off for what seemed an eternity, and when he awoke, he felt well enough to take on his homework assignment. In twenty minutes, he was all done.

Max tore off to the kitchen. His mother and Tommy were there discussing the school day. "We are leaving in ten minutes," his mother said, then she resumed the conversation with Tommy.

"Mommy, is it possible for shadows to form from nothing?" Tommy asked. Max could hear the confusion in his little brother's voice.

"Of course not. There is always light and an object blocking that light, causing the shadow. Why bring up such an odd question?" she replied.

"Oh, I don't know. I thought I saw a shadow formed from nothing, kind of stalking me," Tommy said. "It was there when I was in my bus riding to and from school, at recess, in gym, and just now."

Mrs. Weston's face changed from a little, joyful grin to an unhappy stare. "Stop with such strange and impossible speculations this instant, Tommy James Weston," she yelled.

She uttered not a word more as they got in the car and drove to the pool. Max knew what Tommy was saying was true. He had seen it. And Elzara had told him. The Nightmare, who Max had thought was unreal, had spoken the truth. He felt pity for his brother. Yet a wave of relief flowed through Max's body, assured that the Nightmare was real. And he now knew he wasn't the only one who had seen the uncaused shadow. A small tingle in his heart told him there was a prolonged journey ahead of him.

It was 9:31 p.m., which meant bedtime and hopefully another encounter with the Nightmare for Max. He had been waiting for the night. He felt the urgency to know what the uncaused shadow really was. Max thought the only one that could explain would be Elzara.

He kissed his parents good night and executed Tommy's difficult secret handshake, a bedtime ritual. Max burrowed under his wool quilt and awaited the appearance of the Nightmare, Elzara. Ten minutes passed by, and they felt like the longest ten minutes in Max's life.

Nothing. Just as Max's confidence in the Nightmare's being real narrowed, a red glow appeared, followed by a shot of fire in every direction, nearly singeing the walls. There appeared the horse with its beautiful, fiery, reddish-orange tail.

Fire shot out Elzara's nostrils. "Hello, Max Weston. I am glad to see you again. I feel you are in need of an answer to a question of yours, are you not?" Elzara asked as her flame wings retreated to her side.

"Yes, I do have a question. Throughout the day I have seen an uncaused shadow. It had wings and—"

"What you are describing to me is a Shadowan," interrupted Elzara. "This Shadowan is responsible for watching your every move and alerting others of its kind when it is the right time to leap upon your soul and rip it out. But I won't let that happen to you. I will protect you and guard you from the Shadowa and will assist you in changing your family and the world."

"I'm glad to know that," Max whispered sarcastically to himself. *Now they want to rip my soul out*, he thought. *I thought they only wanted to conquer Earth. But ripping my soul out?* "What will happen if they tear my soul out? How will I act or feel?"

Elzara neighed. "Well, I hope I guard you well enough so you won't have to feel or experience being a Soulless. You can't touch, smell, taste, see, or hear anything. Your brain is dysfunctional. It's as though you are dead, though awake within your being. You leave your dysfunctional body, and you are now a spirit, a poltergeist. This also makes your extremities and muscles dysfunctional and immobilized.

But after being a Soulless for a decade or so, you regain your senses except for sight. But by then you would have become chained to the indestructible manacles of the Shadowa."

Max felt as though those words had penetrated through to his heart and bumped right into it, causing an irregular heartbeat and causing his lungs to halt. For a split second, he lost his breath, but he soon regained it and the beat and rhythm to his heart normalized. "Does that mean I am paralyzed?" Max queried, though not really wanting to know the answer.

"Yes," Elzara said as she closed her eyes.

Max felt a tear roll down his cheek. He didn't want this fate. He needed to change his ways so he and his family could escape the deadening grip of the Shadowa. There had to be more to life than being a Soulless. He knew in his heart that there was more … it meant being a Light Soul. But could he make the change and follow all the demands of being a Light Soul? Could he give himself entirely to this different way of living, of hoping in times of joy and distress?

Max wiped the tear from his face as Elzara neighed, "Climb onto my back, and I will take you on an excursion. Hold on tight; this could be a bumpy ride."

As he straddled onto her back, Max noticed a bright light beaming toward the window. It beamed out of Elzara's eyes. Suddenly the whole left side of the wall was gone, and she took off into the gray-blue sky. He held on for dear life.

Max gripped Elzara's black mane as she weaved her way through the night sky.

"Wow, this is amazing! We are so high up in the sky, the stars look so bright, and the buildings below are so small," Max said to Elzara, still clutching her mane.

"Yes," she neighed, "it's a beautiful sight. Back on my star planet, we have many stars in orbit around us. We are too far from the sun, so we get most of our luminous light from the stars at night. And in the day, our star, Trepiti, glows magnificently."

"Where is your planet located?" Max queried.

"Well, it is near your planet Neptune. It is pretty cold in the winter, but the light from our planet keeps us warm."

Max wondered if he, from Earth, could see the star Trepiti. He was amazed that there was life on another planet besides Earth. *How come our scientists can't find life on another planet or star?* thought Max.

Max and Elzara were still high in the air when suddenly something or someone nearly hit Max off Elzara's back. "Whoaaaaa!" Max yelled, attempting to recover his grip on Elzara's mane. The thing was now tugging on Max's arm, intending to throw Max off Elzara. Elzara swerved left to right, trying to loosen the thing's grip. It didn't work. Struggling against the creature, Max yelled, "What is this thing!?" He now felt the thing's sharp nails pierce his skin and blood trickle down his arm. His legs were clutched tightly to Elzara's back.

Elzara neighed, "It is a Shadowan."

The words came out with a chilling feeling to them. They had encountered a Shadowan! It was simultaneously exciting and frightening to Max.

The Shadowan was invisible—at least to Max, who could not see the creature tugging on his arm. Still struggling, Max used his free arm to attempt to punch the evil creature, but unsurprisingly he missed. He again attempted to punch and this time hit his target. Once Max's knuckles touched the vile thing, the Shadowan revealed itself. It was the most horrifying thing Max had ever seen, worse even than anything from a horror movie. It wore a black and red gown, with yellow eyes unveiled and long nails. He knew it had wings from Elzara's description, but he couldn't see them.

Max paused in horror as Elzara, still in flight, turned her head around and shot out fire from her mouth at the ugly Shadowan. The Shadowan was hit by the fire and was burnt on its side. It loosened its grip and fell, shrieking in pain.

We defeated the Shadowan, Max thought.

"Don't underestimate a Shadowan. They are one of the slyest tricksters there are. When you believe you have finished them, the unthinkable may happen. So keep watch!" Elzara said, gazing around alertly.

"Where are you taking me again?" Max asked, for it was surely past 10:30 p.m. His mother usually scanned the house at midnight to check on Max and Tommy and to see if anybody unknown was lurking about. Max thought it was a sign of paranoia.

"We're going to see some other Dark Souls and Nightmares," the mare answered.

Those words were reassuring to Max; somehow it was comforting to know that he was not the only Dark Soul. "Oh, are my friends Dark Souls?"

"Neither Craig nor Leah are Dark Souls," Elzara answered.

Max's head drooped down in thought. *None of my friends are Dark Souls. That is good for them. They must live different li—*

His thoughts were interrupted as he was pummeled off Elzara's back. Falling, he realized what was now holding him. It was the Shadowan they had encountered just a few minutes ago.

Is this the end of me? Is this how I am to die? were the thoughts that raced through Max's mind. Fear was at its highest level. His heart raced frantically. He just closed his eyes and hoped for the best. He even said a quick prayer.

Still in the sky, Elzara chased after the Shadowan and Max like a cat after a mouse. Her fiery wings flapped faster and faster as she tried to save the one she was assigned to protect. If she didn't get there in time, her mission would be a failure, and another soul would be taken.

Tears poured down Max's cheeks as he fell in the grip of the monster. He felt as though he hadn't lived life as it was supposed be lived. The Shadowan suddenly let Max go as they swooped close to ground. This was it. Max had never thought his death would be like this. He braced himself. He could feel the ground below him nearing quickly.

Elzara dove past the Shadowan, wings fluttering fast. She knew it couldn't end like this for Max. He was young, and she knew he had potential in changing his fate and the world's. Her heartbeat echoed that of Max—frantic and frenzied.

3

DARK SOULS

Suddenly Max felt himself hanging onto something. He gradually managed to open his eyes. He gazed around, unaware of his surroundings, as he pushed himself up on his forearms and felt the long, silky mane against his elbow. It was a horse. It was Elzara! Through his joy, he managed to shout, "You saved me!"

"Yes, I saved you." Elzara's words came out with both triumph and fatigue. "Hold on tight, we're going for a ride."

"Okay! But where to?" Max was overjoyed to still be living, to still be breathing.

"We are going to the state of Ohio."

Ohio, Max thought. *That is far from home*. A hint of anxiousness crept into Max's mind.

Max and Elzara took flight again, and not much later they landed on a rooftop. No one would be able to see the horse and the child on this roof, for in the little town there were very few street lights and Elzara dimmed her flames. Max climbed off Elzara and steadily walked to the edge of the roof to see if any lights were on in the house. There were, in the second-floor room.

Max climbed back onto Elzara and they slowly drifted to the second-floor window. Then Elzara vanished the wall and they entered the room.

In the room stood a young, brunette girl with Hello Kitty pajamas, her hands clasped together on her lap. Beside her was a horse. To Max, they looked like they were anxiously waiting for something or someone. Perhaps Elzara and himself.

"Good. Who have you brought with you, Elzara?" the Nightmare queried. She was whitish-gold and had a jet-black mane. Her wings were made of thunderbolts, and she had a tail of static that seemed like, if touched, could shock you entirely. Sparks shot out of her nostrils.

"I have brought the one I am supposed to guard, Max Weston," replied Elzara.

"How nice it is to meet you, Max. I am Vexa, a Nightmare like Elzara, only I have lightning powers. And this is who I am guarding, Melanie Prattle." The girl waved slowly at Max, and he returned it.

The two Nightmares began speaking about something, a crystal. Meanwhile, Melanie spoke in a sweet voice, "Hi, Max. I guess you are a Dark Soul like me?" Her hazel eyes showed her embarrassment that she was a Dark Soul.

Max nodded, though he hated that it was true. He couldn't believe that he and this pretty girl were Dark Souls. "I am thirteen years old. How old are you?" He felt himself blush when he asked the question. He was just trying to extend the conversation. He didn't want to just stand with Melanie in a deep silence.

Melanie answered, "I am twelve."

"Cool. Have you seen a Shadowan?"

"No, but Vexa described one to me."

"Oh, well I did." Max felt proud and stood erect. "Elzara and I fought one up in the sky. It was magnificent, although it was also terrifying."

"Wow!" exclaimed Melanie, eyes wide in amazement.

"No more getting to know each other for now," Vexa said, looking at the two children. "We are going to retrieve the Crystal of Spei. It has indescribable potency and is capable of bringing brightness to dark worlds."

"Where is this Crystal of Spei?" asked Melanie in a clueless tone.

"What does *spei* mean? And is it even a word?" Max queried.

"*Spei* is the Latin word for *hope*. The Crystal of Spei is the Crystal of Hope in English," responded Elzara. "Its name is not spurious, for it really does instill hope. Some say it has healing powers—not for physical healing, but for spiritual healing. And its location is rumored to be in the Himalayan foothills in Pakistan. It was seen by Ruber, the queen of the Nightmares, as she licked the blue salts on the ground. She was in a team of horses that was part of Alexander the Great's army. Nearby was a cave into which Ruber wandered. As she meandered deeper into the cave, she noticed a crystal emanating with several colors: black, crimson, and then white. It violently shook on the ground. Ruber knew it was unlike any other beautiful crystal. This one was special, and because it was special, she hid it far away, deep in another cave in the jarring foothills and away from Alexander and Bedouins."

"We have no time to spare," Vexa explained. "We can't still be on this journey when sun rises, or we will disappear. We must find the crystal now, or the forces of the Shadowa will become stronger. Soon they will be able to take all the lives of the Dark Souls. With every Dark Soul, they become stronger and more voracious."

Melanie and Max climbed onto their Nightmares. They took off into the night, aware of the dangerous journey that lay ahead. What would their parents and siblings think? Would they be worried?

Max and Melanie were pondering about the journey halfway across the world. Would they return home to their parents? Would they complete the voyage that will determine mankind's survival? With nothing else to do during the ride, Max and Melanie soon fell asleep on the backs of their guardians.

Max woke up to a sweet, tranquil voice. "Wake up, Max. Wake up."

The boy opened his eyes and observed his surroundings. There were trees. Many leaves rustled in a light zephyr. He looked at the ground, wet with dew. An abundance of large rocks were set on the ground, with moss sprawled all over their fronts. He stared at the sun, penetrating through the limbs and branches of the trees. He was forced to look away, for the sun hurt his eyes, leaving prints of kaleidoscopic colors in his sight.

"Thank goodness you're up." Melanie released a sigh of relief. "I felt so alone, and I heard scary noises."

Max noticed that his Nightmare, Elzara, was not present. "Where are Elzara and Vexa?"

Melanie looked up through the trees at the sun. "It is daytime." She looked at Max. "The Nightmares only show themselves at night, remember?"

The two decided to wait for Elzara and Vexa. They didn't know how long it would take for the sun to retreat and the moon to rise, along with the stars. The exact time was unknown to the two of them.

After a while, they felt lonely and frail. Their only sense of protection wwere the Nightmares and they were gone. Max and Melanie knew not any fighting techniques to protect them in sheer suspicion. Max had done Boy Scouts for a while until the "incident" when he felt like there was no possible way to survive. And he didn't remember much either. Melanie was not one for the great outdoors so her knowledge was low. Waiting felt like the only logical thing to do.

They waited and waited as the day went on sluggishly. Patience was wearing thin for the two children. Each minute felt like a millennium. Max became livid. "Do they believe we can fend for ourselves?" he asked.

The image of the Shadowan he had seen the night before raced through his mind. He closed his eyes tightly, hoping to make it disappear. The image managed to slowly fade away, but Max was still worried about being alone without his guardian. It was Elzara who had warned him that he was living life by routine. It was she who had protected him from the vile Shadowan, and it was she who had saved him from falling. "A Shadowan could come any minute and suck our souls with ease," he said, worried.

The wind began to pick up. It grew colder with every gust. "We need to build a fire if we want to stay warm," Max suggested.

Melanie nodded, shivering. "We ought to look for some wood." The two walked together into the depths of the forest.

The sunbeams seldom made it through the thick branches of the dark and dense forest. The two could barely see five feet ahead of them. Max knew it was morning, but it was considerably dark. He and Melanie picked up large twigs and branches, nestling them in their arms. Melanie suddenly yelped, "Ouch!" She discontinued her picking up twigs for she had received a painful splinter on her right index finger. She switched to just pointing out sticks and twigs that lay around to be helpful for Max.

Without warning something moved behind a gnarled oak tree. Max and Melanie both froze in their stances as leaves rustled.

Tense, Max dropped his armful of sticks, making noise. That sudden movement was a mistake.

Another noise came from another direction. They turned again toward the noise. Silence. Max didn't dare move a muscle this time. What if the thing was behind him? He tried to persuade himself that whatever thing that was making the noise wasn't, but he couldn't.

They heard it another sound and suddenly saw it in front of them—a horrible, savage Shadowan! The creature opened its mouth wide, showing its sharp, deadly fangs. The Shadowan hissed repulsively. It gripped Max by the arm and pulled him close to its hideous face. Its yellow eyes with pin-sized pupils stared back at Max. It licked its lips as it wiggled its snakelike tongue in anticipation.

Melanie grabbed a stone by the wayside and flung it at the Shadowan's head. The creature lost its grip on Max and drew back. The ugly creature eyed Melanie and hissed as it crept slowly in her direction.

The Shadowan's body pulsated rhythmically, and it seemed to be charging up power inside its chest. Then its thorax split open, revealing a ball of darkness. The spinning ball of darkness came hurtling toward Melanie. She averted the dark energy ball with the agility of a track runner and hid behind a giant spruce. The trunk of the tree must have been eighteen inches thick, but it was sliced nearly completely through by the energy.

The black-clad Shadowan hissed once more, piercing the early morning stillness. It charged up another dark ball of energy in its chest. He flew up into the air and aimed at Melanie, who was frozen in position.

Max saw this and rushed to Melanie. The creature ejected the energy ball from its midsection. Trepidation remained in the dimly lit forest.

"Noooo!" shouted Max, tackling Melanie like a linebacker in football. The bold, risky act saved Melanie from injury, perhaps death, as the energy ball missed its target.

Max quickly picked up a huge branch with both of his arms. He swung it with all his strength, releasing it at just the right moment to hit his target's foot as the Shadowan floated ten feet in the air. The Shadowan shrieked in pain, but it didn't let up. Why should it? No Nightmare was present to protect the two young children. It knew they were defenseless against its powers.

The ugly beast floated slowly to the Earth. The Shadowan's every movement was as graceful and fluid as a calculating leopard stalking its prey softly. The savage stuck its lethal claws out at Max, who retreated quickly but tripped over a smutty stone. He was helpless now. He knew that the Shadowan would easily devour his soul, without a doubt.

The Shadowan loomed over Max. Its chest opened again, not attempting to fire an energy ball, though. Max could see Melanie's face through the hole, the edges of which began to whirr. It began to suck Max's soul. Max lost his breath and—

At that moment Melanie pelted the Shadowan with a rock. The Shadowan quickly released its grip on Max and dropped onto its victim's now-unconscious body. Melanie shoved the savage off Max. She stared at it intently and warily, but the Shadowan just disintegrated into black dust.

Max's senses returned. He heard a soft whimper. Where was it coming from? He tried to open his eyes but failed to. He felt drops of water falling on his forehead. *Tears*, Max thought. He tried to stand up but failed, for his legs were numb. He attempted to open his eyes again. Failure. *They are glued shut*, Max thought.

The crying stopped.

Suddenly, Max's life flashed before his eyes. The memory of his young childhood brought joy to him, but that joy was quickly erased as he viewed the memory of "the incident." He was also thinking of his parents, of Elzara and Vexa, and of the Shadowa. What were his parents doing? Were they looking for him? Were they panicking? Had they informed the police? Max felt clueless. He couldn't answer any of these questions, which lingered in his mind like dark clouds after a tumultuous storm.

"Max," said a soft, gentle voice. "Max, you moved! You are alive! Can you hear me?"

Max did hear. He tried to raise his hand and give a thumbs-up to notify that he had heard, but his arm was just as numb as his legs. He tried again, this time raising his hand a whole two inches. Not much, but a good start. He was determined to raise his hand, and with much effort, he did it. Now he clenched his hand into a fist, thumb stuck out. Melanie bent down and laid her head on Max's chest. She whispered kind and encouraging words. "Yes," the girl shouted, "you did hear me!"

It was evident to Max that she was ecstatic. He was now even more resolute in successfully standing up and opening his eyelids. He tried and effortlessly stood up. It was as though a surplus of strength had just gushed out of him. Now he was determined to open the eyes. *I* will *open my eyes*, he thought. *I will*. Max struggled at first, but with not so much ease, he finally did open them. He saw the young girl. The beautiful girl. Melanie. Melanie's eyes were red and puffy from crying.

"Max," she exclaimed exuberantly, giving Max a big hug.

The sun crept lower and lower in the sky, turning it a purplish-orange hue that looked glorious. The altocumulus clouds were scattered about the heavens like pink exhaust fumes from a rocket ship. Max and Melanie gathered acorns and twigs from the forest to start a fire and relieve themselves of their hunger. Max started the fire, remembering his Boy Scout rules. Melanie waited anxiously for the acorns to roast.

Max had never experienced life in the wilderness, nor had Melanie. He was freezing and hungry. The fire was of minimal warmth. It didn't keep his hands warm. No wonder he'd quit Boy Scouts, he pondered.

Melanie divided the number of acorns evenly and handed Max half. Although they had only nine acorns apiece, at least it was better than nothing. Thoughts of how the homeless and poor must survive sprang up in Max's mind.

The sun set, which meant Max's and Melanie's Nightmares would appear soon. They would be worry free, protected, and cared for. Finally.

Soon they heard a neigh from the forest. Max turned and stood up, already knowing who the noise was coming from. Melanie stood too when another neigh sounded, this time with a voice succeeding it. Max thought Vexa and Elzara were speaking to each other. But when a horse jumped out of the forest, the two children saw a boy on an unknown Nightmare's back.

The horse noticed the two children, who looked startled, if not dejected. "Hello, and who are you two?" the Nightmare asked with leaves cascading out its nostrils. She had a green tint in every taupe hair, and white spots polka-dotted her everywhere.

Max was disappointed. He thought it had been Elzara neighing. He tried not to show the dejection he felt. "I am Max Weston." He said, quizzically.

Melanie's voice followed. "I am Melanie Prattle." She pushed her brunette hair from her eyes.

"Ahhh, I am glad to meet you. I am Delveen, a vine Nightmare. I am guarding Justin Smith, a Dark Soul."

The boy waved. His dark skin looking like gold in the sun's last rays. He also had jet-black hair similar to Vexa's mane and was also very tall. He had a bag tied around his back and was barefoot. He looked as though he was kind, brave, and spirited.

Max stared at the vine Nightmare, Delveen, for a reasonably long time. *A vine Nightmare; that is … different*, Max thought. *But where are Elzara and Vexa? Where could they be?*

"Are you two Dark Souls?" Delveen asked.

"Desolately, yes," Max replied, imitating Elzara. Melanie nodded, ashamed of the truth.

"Then excuse me if I ask where your Nightmares are?" Delveen asked incredulously.

"We don't know," Melanie answered. "but we believe that the sun and daylight vanished them. But now that we can hardly see the sun and night is falling, we are extremely worried."

And just as Melanie finished her sentence, there stood in front of the three children and the Nightmare both Elzara and Vexa, fire and lightning manes flowing smoothly in the soft zephyrs.

4

THE PATH OF THE POLTERGEISTS

"Welcome, friend. I can't remember the last time I saw you," Elzara said ruefully. "I regret the busyness that has obstructed our friendship."

"I accept the apology, friend. I, too, have been busy," Delveen said. "How are you, Vexa? Which child is yours?"

"I guard the quiet girl, Melanie, and I am well," Vexa answered.

"And you, Elzara?"

"I guard Max, the eager lad," Elzara said. "We are looking for the Crystal of Spei."

"We, too, are searching for the crystal," said Delveen.

"We can search together," said Melanie. "It'll be an easier find with more eyes on the lookout."

"Great idea," said Vexa. "Let's get going, for time is unstoppable, and every minute counts."

Thus Max, Melanie, and Justin took off on their Nightmares into the night sky on their journey westward to the Eastern Hemisphere.

During the flight, the three children began talking about their lives and encounters with the Shadowa. "Yes, it was awesome," Max explained, proud of his encounter with the Shadowa and trying to seem brave. "And I fell, and Elzara caught me on her back."

Justin and Melanie were both fascinated with every word that came from Max's mouth. "Falling from the sky must've been scary, wasn't it?" Justin queried.

"Well, it was pretty frightening. I thought it was the end of me, to tell you the truth," Max answered. *Oh, boy was it frightening*, thought Max. "But somehow knowing I had Elzara with me made the fright go away. She is so strong and confident."

As the conversation faded, they looked at the stars. The stars looked like tiny holes in the black blanket of a sky. They saw the Big Dipper, Betelgeuse, and the Little Dipper as they soared through the open, tranquil night air.

Soon they were caught in a deep sleep.

Max awoke to the sound of talking. He lifted his head up from Elzara's back and looked around at his surroundings. The black night made picking out details a complicated task. Behind him was a looming structure similar to a house. Next to the house-like edifice was a smaller, flat structure. Max could hear the occasional moos and oinks echoing from the flat building. *It must be a stable*, thought Max. These obnoxious noises made Max wonder how farmers maintained sanity while around the farm animals.

"Where are we?" Max asked drowsily.

"In a state called Nebraska," Elzara answered. "We landed here to rest our wings."

Max was ecstatic to be headed on this journey. Retrieving the crystal meant that the race of the Shadowa would be extinguished. There would be no more suffering or worrying over the forces of evil. Though Dark Souls and Light Souls would still exist, Max wouldn't be killed for being a Dark Soul.

Melanie woke up to Justin's snoring. She reached for him and nudged. Justin almost fell off of Delveen's back.

"What was that for?" asked Justin tiredly.

"That was for your snoring," Melanie said sternly.

"Where are we?" Justin asked.

"Nebraska," Delveen's voice boomed, as if exhausted from the journey.

"What? I am too far from home! I should not be here. I should be in bed in my house in Indianapolis." Justin panicked.

"Calm down, Justin, we'll be okay," Delveen said soothingly. "Remember, I am here to guide you and won't let you falter as long as you listen to me."

The group began walking, Elzara leading the way with her radiant glow of fire snorting out to light the path. She looked like a leader, too, standing erect with a gait so fluid. She seemed like she knew where she was headed.

Max paused, and so did the Nightmares and other Dark Souls. They were heading from plains into a forest when Max began hearing slight moans and groans. Now everyone hearing the eerie noises, the three Dark Souls came closer to their Nightmares as they started to creep deeper into the forest. What if these moans and groans were of the Shadowa? Or was it a dying animal? Perhaps a wounded Nightmare? They continued on their way cautiously.

As they entered the daunting forest, green light glowed menacingly, yet vibrantly. Max was the most cautious of all, tiptoeing lightly. His hands were on Elzara's side the whole time. Now they all could see where the moaning was coming from. Their pathway was lit by green beings.

The beings were a crowd of green spirits. Their moans were horrendous and unpleasant to the ear. They seemed to be craving for something, but so unhopeful. Their moans echoed in incessant misery. The sound altogether was like a symphony of forbidden and ill-favored music so highly strung it made your ears bleed.

"What are you guys?" said Max, eager for answers.

"We are spirits of the Dark Souls," answered a green, translucent spirit. Its reply sounded like the growl of a stomach. "Our fleshy forms have been conquered by the wicked and savage Shadowa."

Disbelief and horror shot through Max's veins along with his blood. If he were conquered by a Shadowan, would he end up here with these green, fleshless, moaning spirits? The only optimistic answer to this fear-striking question was to avoid being defeated by a Shadowan.

"Where are we?" Melanie asked.

"You are now on the Path of the Poltergeists," moaned another specter.

Elzara flared fire through her nostrils. "You are Soulless, right?"

"Yes. We are the spirits of the ones conquered by the evil ones. And every minute that passes, another group of Shadowa is born. They are now greater than ever, in strength and in numbers. They will now come not alone, but in groups to conquer the Dark Souls. This is extremely sad news. You, Dark Souls, be on your guard. Do not let the things of this world numb and engross you." The spirit was shaking horribly in fear.

They continued through the narrow pathway, bounded on each

side by emerald poltergeists and with enormous trees ominously hanging over them. A specter reached out to Justin, who responded by leaping out of reach. "Be very aware of everything around you," screeched the sea-green ghost. Justin looked terrified. By the look on his dark face, he was surely aware of everything around him. "Why don't you spirits leave this dreadful and spooky place?" he asked shakily.

The translucent spirit showed a chain connected to its feet and wriggled it for the Nightmares and Dark Souls. "We are eternally imprisoned. There is nothing we can do to escape. We can't even fade through these chains. These eternal chains are unbreakable."

"Who chained you?" Max asked.

"The dreadful Shadowa," said the poltergeist.

They moved along this sad, mournful path, each lost in thought. The poltergeists moaned continuously. Max, Melanie, and Justin had so many worries of what would become of them if defeated by the Shadowa. All hope seemed to have vanished. They all held their heads down in thought and in fear.

The jade passageway felt endless to the three Dark Souls. They would like nothing more than to be at home in their mothers' comforting embraces. The horrible news they'd learned, these past few days, that they must journey to save their future from being taken away, was too strong for their young minds. Learning that they were Dark Souls was too sudden. It was hard to grasp that one day you could be alive and the next dead as a Soulless.

The Path of the Poltergeists finally ended, leading them into a non-green, pathless forest. Exiting the boisterous pathway, silence bound the group of kids and Nightmares. The trees looked to Max like the clawed hands of a Shadowan reaching for his flesh. They moved cautiously through the fear-provoking, bloodcurdling forest, preparing themselves for any spontaneous meeting they might have with the malevolent Shadowa.

5

IN THE CAVERN

The wind began to howl as the Nightmares and their Dark Souls continued through the eerie forest. The chill of the wind made them shiver, like when the browning leaves shiver to the invigorating autumn breezes. They were all thinking and wondering. Quiet ruled the night, although an occasional owl screech and rustling of a shrub cracked the silent barrier.

"Come now, climb onto our backs," uttered Elzara as they stepped out from the trees at long last.

The Dark Souls climbed onto their Nightmares, who took off into the night, racing into the black of the sky.

Max's legs gradually became numb from sitting on Elzara's back for an extended time. All through the night, he marveled at the brightly lit stars. They were so radiant and marvelous that they helped take his mind off his aching legs.

Max also marveled at the flames spurting from Elzara's nostrils, spurting out the same as her tail and as her wonderful wings. He was awestruck by the way she loved him and had vowed to keep him safe.

He also thought about the long, scary, but incredible journey they were on. Max wondered how he had made it this far. He felt absolutely dependent on Elzara, as defenseless as a newly born babe. He had neither flames nor wings nor hooves of wondrous power. He was as frail as a leaf.

Elzara's fire wings kept Max warm also, although the wind was chilly. That led to a warm, comfortable nap.

Max woke up and immediately observed the sky. The sky was as black as black can be, except for the bright stars and huge moon to lighten the sea of darkness. *Still nighttime. Good*, Max thought sleepily. He saw Elzara's flames sizzling, Vexa's static zap, and Delveen's vines slithering about. *They're amazing. They can do anything*, Max thought to himself.

"Good to see you awake, Max. We are now preparing to land in California," neighed Elzara. "We are getting closer."

As the pack dove toward the ground, Max felt like he was skydiving. Although he had never experienced it, he did see Craig's older sister do it. It looked frightening and that was what Max felt.

Soon they landed, and then they rested.

Max awoke. The sun was lowering in the distance. He gazed around. Ahead he saw mountain peaks.

Max sat on a huge boulder in which lay near a lake. He mused about how long it would take them to reach the Himalaya foothills. He wondered if the Shadowa were going to delay their journey.

He took a smooth pebble and threw it into the lake, and it sunk quickly. Would the voyage for the Crystal of Spei be like the pebble, a failure from the start? Max took another pebble and flung it into the lake. It skipped three times before sinking. Would the journey be like this pebble, perfect and without hardships? Max suggested that it would be like the pebble that skipped. He wanted this journey to be a success.

Night defeated the last strands of day. Max headed back to where Melanie and Justin were. He climbed up onto a rock and then another. He took his time to make out objects in the dark. He made it to them who weren't sleeping but awake with all three Nightmares with them.

"Nice to see you again, Max," said Elzara, her flames shining in the night. "We must move along. Climb on me."

Max walked toward Elzara and sat on her back. The whole group took off into the starless night. The journey resumed.

Max was beginning to doze off. He had recently been thinking about home. He was beginning to feel homesick. He missed his family and yearned to be in his warm bed. He had never been by himself since the "incident" in fear of the same results occurring.

"We are now flying over the Hawaiian Islands," voiced Elzara, turning her head slightly to see Max.

Hawaii, Max thought, *Never thought I would ever visit here.*

"Max, are you homesick?" asked Elzara, still flying through the darkness.

Max hesitated. "Yes," he said, finally, "how did you know?"

"I could feel it in you. You should not be homesick. We will return you home."

"Yeah, but wouldn't they be worrying about *me*? A couple of days have passed since, wouldn't my family be scared about my disappearance?"

"No, we've taken care of it," Elzara said.

Max was incredulous. "But how?"

"Do you doubt us?"

Max didn't reply. Why prolong the conversation when Elzara would not disclose any more information? Of course he didn't doubt them. They were horses with flames, lightning bolts, and vines. Who would doubt them?

Max just sat, his numb legs dangling freely, thinking. But thinking soon led to sleeping.

Max woke up on his Nightmare's back. It was still night, and the moon shined brighter than usual. Its silver light permitted Max to see the rest of the group. They were no longer flying but were walking.

"Where are we?" Max queried, gazing at the moonlit hills.

"We are in the Himalayan foothills in Bhutan. The Crystal of Spei is here," Elzara answered.

They were in Asia. A long way from the United States of America. It didn't help to know Max was farther from home; it made it worse.

"Let's hurry. The time zone of Bhutan has given us an extra night so let not waste it," said Vexa to Max's left.

"Good idea," agreed Delveen to Max's right. The three Dark Souls were gazing at the moonlit glens dreamily.

They took off again, flying through valleys and gliding over small bodies of water. The different and varied features of the land made Max marvel. Hills, valleys, and plateaus—it was all beautiful. It seemed almost magical.

They flew close to the ground so that they would be able to see the cave in which Ruber had hidden the crystal. As they skimmed over the diverse terrain, something caught Elzara's eye. She saw two moving things near a dark patch in the snowy mountainside. At first she thought they were human, but with a second careful scan, she realized they were Shadowa.

"It is that cave," Elzara said, gliding toward the dark hole in a foothill.

"How can you be sure?" asked Delveen.

"Because two Shadowa walked in, signifying that the Crystal of Spei is probably in there."

Max thought for a moment then said, "How do you know that?"

"I know because the Shadowa are there to stop us from recouping the crystal. If we retrieve it, you three will become Light Souls. The crystal will change you forever."

"So you're telling me," Justin started even as the three descended to the ground, "that there could be an army of Shadowa huddled in that cave and ready to defeat us?"

There was no reply, for as Justin finished his sentence, the group was whopped by an invisible force.

Max, Melanie, and Justin had been dismounted by the blow, and the Nightmares were flung to the left. What had hit them? It was as though an invisible force field had elongated, obstructing the group's path and knocking them away just as they'd hit the ground.

Elzara rolled back onto all fours. "Shadowa!" she yelled. She readied herself and flew quickly to Max. The other Nightmares followed suit, galloping to their Dark Souls.

Max stood up quickly. The invisible Shadowa were hovering

someplace, either over or around them. Who knew? Max was suddenly tackled off his feet, falling to his back with a loud thump. He was slashed on his arm by the Shadowan's talons. He felt something on him, but he couldn't do much but swing a blind punch. He hit nothing but air. The Shadowan started to choke him. He struggled to breathe as he felt for the Shadowan's hands on his neck. He grasped the hands and tried to shake them loose but couldn't. The creature was too strong. The savage's hands constricted Max's trachea still further, stopping Max's breathing. Max strained in a last attempt to survive, feeling his heartbeat slowing down to a monotonous *lub ... dub.*

Elzara charged up a fireball and shot it just above Max's body. It was a direct hit. The savage beast shrieked in pain as it toppled over to the side, becoming visible as it screamed in a violent throe.

Max gasped for air, filling his lungs to capacity. After a few moments, he felt refreshed. He was scared, and his muscles were numb. He had been only seconds away from death.

The group was now prepared for another invisible blow. They gazed around the area. Justin saw a black orb vibrating in the air. He tapped Delveen and pointed to the dark ball, which seemed to be floating. Delveen quickly yelled, "Watch out!"

Everyone ducked for cover or threw themselves to one side. The dark energy orb blasted from where it floated, hurtling toward the group but hitting nothing. A screech of anger resonated. Delveen unraveled a vine from her mouth and shot it forward toward the area where the dark sphere had been. The vine wrapped around something, and Delveen hauled it in. She constricted so tightly that the Shadowan became visible and then shattered into black dust.

"Is that all of them?" asked Max, panting in apprehension.

"We can't be sure," answered Elzara. "There could be an

army of them surrounding us. We can't always know where they are or where they might be."

They started on their trail, everyone on edge. They made it to the entrance of the cave without further incident. The children climbed off their Nightmares and walked softly beside them. Elzara entered the cave first, her fire-blazing wings at ease. The cavern was pitch dark. Flames spurted out Elzara nostrils, providing the only faint light. The rest of the group followed the sputtering, red flames.

Suddenly Elzara halted, everyone stopping around her. "Find sticks," demanded the fire mare. "Wrap some cloth around each, and I'll light them with my flames to make torches so we can spread out more." The Dark Souls found sticks, and each tore a piece of their pajamas off for Elzara to light. They continued on their way, the path now bright.

After they journeyed deeper into the cave, Elzara stopped, turned, and whispered, "There are Shadowa here." She looked behind her and then continued, "I counted three visible ones. Retrieving the Crystal of Spei won't be easy."

Quickly Elzara turned to the Shadowa, who discharged dark spheres from their chests, and charged at them, shooting fireballs at them as she went. Vexa, too, rushed at the vile creatures to aid Elzara. Delveen stayed with the children to fend off any Shadowa that slipped by the other two Nightmares' attack. Sure enough, one eluded the Nightmares, and Delveen grappled it as it tried to reach Justin. She flung it to the ceiling, a stalactite incising the Shadowan through the heart. The monster disintegrated into dust right before their eyes.

Elzara nimbly moved lateral, dodging a dark orb, and fired a fireball. The Shadowan dove to its left and shot another energy ball. Elzara evaded the dark ball by flying over it and aerial dived into the Shadowan, pounding it into a sharp stalagmite. It dissolved into black powder.

Vexa sent a thunderbolt at the last Shadowan. The creature shot a dark sphere at the thunderbolt, causing a mini explosion and halting the course of both shots. Next, Vexa strode toward the demon-like monster and chomped on its hand as it tried to evade the big horse teeth. Yellow blood trickled down like sweat from your brow, and Vexa formed an electric impulse within which traveled through to the Shadowan, shocking it violently. The lifeless creature fell to the ground, shattering into dust.

They continued, climbing over rocks, removing obstacles, and fitting through tight places. Salt crystals were scattered around the grimy floor of the grotto. Max felt an inner happiness replacing his hopeless despondency. He was glad that they were close to retrieving the crystal. Hope would be found. Joy would be present. Everything would be better. But how could Max be hopeful after such a tragic event in which changed his life?

They finally reached the end of the cavern's twists and turns, coming to a wide open space with no other passages leading out of it. Three Shadowa were defending something—something that was glowing vibrantly.

"Is that the Crystal of Spei?" whispered Melanie as they hid in the shadows, unnoticed as the Shadowa were facing the other direction.

"Yes, it is," answered Vexa.

"How do we get it?" Justin murmured, staying close to Delveen.

"Well, we can combat them and then retrieve the crystal, or we can clandestinely snatch it away from them," Elzara whispered in reply.

Max was bewildered. "What does *clandestinely* mean? I am not that good in vocabulary."

"It means stealthily or secretly," replied Elzara. She stopped her flames from jetting out, going into stealth mode.

"Which one should we do?" asked Justin.

"I don't know," said Elzara.

Then, the Shadowa shuffled in place. They turned toward the brightness that came from behind them and spotted their enemies. With a gleam of spite in his yellow eyes, one Shadowan lifted the crystal over its cloaked head. The jewel glowed a deep black, a magnificent red, and then a wholesome white. Without warning the monster then drove the gemstone to the grimy ground with such force that it shattered into three distinct shards with a sound like a glass window sundering after being hit by a baseball.

Shock and a deep rage struck Max, Melanie, and Justin like a whip. "How could they?" Max yelled.

"Will we still be able to become Light Souls?" said Melanie more to herself than to anyone else.

"Those freakish monsters," Justin shouted.

In rage, Justin charged at the Shadowan who had smashed the crystal against the ground and tackled him. His petite body was no match for the enormous brute; he just hung there around the monster's waist like leeches stuck to a man's back. The harassed creature tried to rip Justin off his back, but Justin wouldn't let go. The other two Shadowa removed Justin from their cohort and held him tight.

"Let him go!" Delveen exclaimed, rushing forward with vines flowing out of her nostrils.

The Shadowan cackled like a hyena. "We can't do that," he hissed, letting the Dark Souls hear a Shadowan voice for the first time. "We're going to take him with us."

"Take him where?" Melanie cried.

"Why, to our realm, of course," said the Shadowan. Its voice was sleek and rich and raspy.

"Where is that?" queried Max, the trepidation in his voice surprising him a bit.

"Why, it is above the clouds in the mesosphere. The perfect location to spy out every Dark Soul, for you can't see us, but we see you. How do you think we track you down? If it wasn't for our vital position, we would have to resort to stalking you, which to some can be discernible. You, for instance."

Max could understand now. He'd been able to see the shadows of the Shadowa, like the day on the bus. He could never quite understand what they were at the time, but he'd had an aura that those shadows weren't quite normal. He knew that what he had seen most people couldn't, and then Elzara had come to explain it all.

The first Shadowan charged up a dark sphere from its hands and hurled it at Justin. It didn't hurt him, but rather engulfed him in a bubble of dark energy. It was transparent from the outside, but on the inside it was opaque. Justin hit his fists against the dark bubble but to no avail. Every time he struck it, the others would see on his face an expression of agony, and he would look weak. What was happening to Justin? Was he slowly dying an excruciating death?

"Let him go!" Delveen shouted, now livid. Her vines were standing by, waving in the air like cobras ready to pounce on their prey.

All three Shadowa laughed mockingly. "No can do," said one.

Delveen grunted in a fury. She launched her coiling vines at the three Shadowa. She was able to grasp one, but the vines missed the other two due to their quick dodges. The two escaping ones became invisible, though they abandoned the dark bubble. In rage, Delveen compressed her captive into a limp and lifeless form.

In the midst of the battle, everything was happening so quickly. Everyone was tense. Where would the other two Shadowa reappear?

Delveen galloped to the bubble in which Justin was detained. She used her creepers to try to pierce the bubble but was unsuccessful. She tried once more but with the same result.

Max was suddenly knocked off his feet by something. He knew what it was, though: a Shadowan. Max kicked at the air above him. He hit something, and that something screeched. Max quickly got back onto his feet. The Shadowan he'd kicked was now visible once more.

Elzara hurtled a saucer of fire at the Shadowan. It burned and wailed in suffering, consumed by the red-orange flames. It fell, then it tried to stand up but failed, too badly injured.

Silence—but not for long. A dark sphere came rushing at Melanie, who noticed it a second too late. It thumped her in the chest, causing her heart to skip. She crashed to the ground, black sparks jumping off her body. Vexa galloped to her charge, only to find Melanie frozen. Alive, but frozen.

Another dark ball was launched in Melanie's direction. Vexa saw it, averted it, and then fired a lightning bolt toward where the dark ball had originated. A cry called out, and the creature reappeared. It fell to the ground and shook in a seizure.

Moments later the Shadowan regained control of itself and stood up. It jumped up and began to glow in many different hues— black, navy, violet, and gray. The vile creature gathered the three pieces of the Crystal of Spei and held them in one hand, grasping the dark bubble in the other. Delveen rammed into the Shadowan, but it maintained a strong hold on the bubble, which now also began to flicker many different colors.

"They're warping away!" cried Elzara. She and Vexa dashed toward Justin's bubble.

Delveen grabbed onto the Shadowan and then clutched onto Max, Elzara, Melanie, and Vexa with her long vines.

Then, the cavern was silent and vacant.

6

PURSUIT

Max appeared in a dark room. Elzara stood next to his side, flame tail and wings glimmering. He positioned himself so that he could see from the light from Elzara's tail and scanned the area. Mosaic blocks of dark purple and gunmetal were scattered along the walls. The ceilings were about ten feet high. An eerie light from torches hung from holsters on the wall. The room was scarcely lit.

Melanie and Vexa stood to the left of Max. Melanie was on Vexa's back, limp as a piece of successfully hunted prey. She was slowly fading into unconsciousness.

Delveen was behind Max, her vines long and winding. Her green-tinted, muscle-bound, chestnut horse figure looked magnificent in the eerie light.

They heard a clamor down a corridor. Max twisted to his right. A silhouette of a creature with a big, round sphere suspended in the air lolled on the floor.

"Follow that shadow!" Elzara neighed, galloping after the silhouette, which she knew was the Shadowan and the entrapped Justin. Vexa and Max sprinted behind the flaring mare. Delveen flew just above the floor instead.

The corridor sprouted into an area with three open, arched doorways. Elzara's hooves skidded against the asphalt as she quickly came to a stop. The rest of the caravan came to a halt behind Elzara.

They all stared at the three doors.

"Which do we go through?" asked Max.

Elzara didn't respond promptly. She looked intently at the door on the left, eyes squinting as if looking for the tiniest hint in the faint lighting. Next, she stared at the center passageway, and then to the right. Her ears stood erect in an effort to capture any miniscule sound of movement in the distance. Her ears wriggled slightly as she received the sound waves.

"This way," she finally replied, dashing to the right door. Max kicked his legs into running mode again, following Elzara through the doorway.

Shortly they reached a much larger room, with better lighting than before. It had no doors or passageways, but a spiral staircase rose up in front of them, about twenty stories high. Max scanned up the enormously tall staircase and saw a dark creature on what would be the third story. The creature was dashing up the flight of stairs like a mouse running for dear life from a hunting house cat. The orb, which enclosed Justin, was keeping pace with the Shadowan as if somehow magically connected to the monster.

"Up there," said Max, pointing somewhat skyward toward the spiral staircase. "The Shadowan is going up."

Elzara, Vexa, and Delveen glanced at the ascending corkscrew stairs. "Get on me," Elzara said. Max did so, and the two lifted into the air. Vexa launched immediately after them.

The Shadowan took a hasty glance at its pursuers to see how far down they were, but once he saw them soaring closer, he lifted off also, wings invisible. Elzara's flame wings flapped at warp speed. As the Nightmares came closer, the Shadowan fired shots at Elzara and Max. A dark ball nearly hit Elzara's muzzle. She was taken aback, furious. She flew straight despite the fact that she was scanning the vicinity.

"There are more Shadowa here than we can see," Elzara uttered, warning the others.

Max consumed her words, now searching for any dark ball. He saw two flying toward him like bullets. "Elzara," he yelled, "two from your right!"

Elzara quickly turned her head right and located the incoming enemy spheres. As they came closer, she thrust her body forward to avoid them. More spheres were fired, but with Max's help Elzara and the other Nightmares dodged them deftly. They all showed incredible speed and agility.

The Shadowan with Justin finally made it to the top of the flight of stairs. It appeared tired and winded, but it quickly regained its composure and continued its run down a dark hall with torches. The hall extended all the way until the torches could no longer be seen.

More dark orbs were fired, now several at a time. Twelve rocketed toward Max and Elzara like missiles from a rocket launcher. Elzara couldn't pinpoint them all as they torpedoed closer. Max knew it would take a miracle to escape this life-threatening predicament.

Just then Vexa, with the grayish Melanie on her back, flew up alongside and created an electric force field around Elzara and Max. The dark balls crashed into the force field, unable to penetrate the interior.

After the barrage of dark spheres, Vexa's force field fizzled and then disappeared. Max was flabbergasted at what he had just seen. *That was surely a miracle*, Max thought. The recent occurrences reminded him of the comics he used to read on Saturday mornings. Vexa's force field, indeed, surpassed the comics.

They finally made it to the top of the spiral stairs. Elzara, Max, Delveen, Vexa, and the colorless Melanie all pursued the Shadowan who held Justin in the transparent sphere. Elzara shot a fireball at the running creature. It would have been a perfect hit if the Shadowan hadn't suddenly rolled lateral in a sense of the fireball nearing. It then made a quick turn.

The dark hall with torches where they were looked just like the area where they had started. Elzara came to the place where the savage had turned. She turned also. It was pitch black down this path. Elzara's flame and Vexa's spark tail offered the only light. The narrow pathway made Max uncomfortable. He had never had any symptoms of claustrophobia before, but he sure did now.

They finally came out into a large room, towering high. There were windows to let in some light. It was chillier in the room, too, perhaps from the change in altitude after climbing twenty stories' worth of stairs. There was a band of Shadowa at the end of the room. They stood still, waiting. In their midst was Justin, still trapped in the dark but transparent ball.

"Hello there," said a menacing Shadowan, dressed in a red gown rather the black of the Shadowa behind him. A menacing smirk spread across his unveiled and grotesque face from ear to ear.

7

THE COMPROMISE

"Just give him back!" shouted Delveen.

The lead Shadowan's smirk was replaced by a frown. "Not one for salutations, I see," he voiced.

Delveen grunted. She stamped in fury, upset at the reply. "Release the boy!"

Max looked at Melanie, who was being cared for by Vexa. Her grayness was sickening. Vexa looked as though she did not know what to do. "What's going to happen to her? Will she be okay?" Max queried as he knelt with Vexa.

"I am not sure." Vexa looked dejected. "This is a very bizarre occurrence. If hit with a dark energy ball, one's heart doesn't continue beating afterward, leaving one in a state of paralysis ... usually. Death steals your life on contact. The Shadowan must have weakened the ball by changing his initial intention with it, hence making the dark energy ball not kill Melanie but only immobilize her."

"Bravo, Bravo," the superior Shadowan chortled. "You figured it out. I can return her to her natural state and release the boy if you are willing to negotiate ... a compromise. The girl—"

"Never will we negotiate with you vile creatures!" Delveen shouted, interrupting him.

But Elzara was more willing to listen to what the savage had to say. "Quiet, Delveen. Let's hear him out."

"As I was saying," the red-clad monster said, looking pleased, "the girl will be returned to perfect condition if a Nightmare lays down her life for the lass. And the dark-skinned boy will be released if the crystal remains ours. Deal?"

Max thought this bargain was absurd. Would the Nightmares actually agree to this horrid compromise? He knew that being Dark Souls, that would still kill Melanie, in a sense, including himself and Justin.

Elzara's face took on a new look as her eyebrows pinched in deep contemplation. Then her face seemed to come to life. "We agree."

Shock crowded Max's head. *What? He thought. How could you agree to such a lunatic deal?*

"No, *you* agree" Delveen sounded off furiously. "We should at least talk it over and put it to a vote. Who will sacrifice her life to save Melanie, anyway?"

"I will," Elzara uttered.

Max froze stiff, as though he'd heard a creepy noise in the middle of the night. Tears began to build up in his eyes. *No*, he thought. *She mustn't. It's like suicide.*

But then he thought of Melanie. The girl who was in her Hello Kitty pajamas accompanying him through the forest when their Nightmares weren't present. The girl with a smile that made him flush.

At that moment, Vexa said, "No, I will sacrifice my life for my Dark Soul. She is my responsibility, so I ought to do it." Valor was audible in her voice, and also a slight quiver of sadness.

"But—" Delveen started.

"No, Melanie is my responsibility. It will be me who will be the sacrifice."

Max's mind finished processing the disturbing information. It was like a massive tidal wave crashing down on his scrawny little body.

"Wonderful," announced the Shadowan leader to the rest of his cohorts, a large smile widening on his monstrous face.

Vexa trotted slowly toward the band of black creatures, then she paused and turned toward Elzara, Max, Delveen, and the unconscious Melanie. Although her horse facial expressions were unlike humans', Max could tell she was downhearted. Her eyes quivered, her whole face trembling. "Friends, I bid thee farewell. This is something I must do. The Divinity must have foreordained it to be," she said, voice shaking as she slowly turned and trotted at a snail's pace to the Shadowa.

"Good-bye," Max cried, tears streaming down his round cheeks. This wasn't what he thought would happen. Why couldn't they have retrieved the Crystal of Spei and returned home safe and sound, hale and hearty? Now Vexa had to die to save Melanie? How could this be?

When Vexa reached the leader of the creatures, who still wore his broad smile, the red-dressed leader said, "This will be quick, so you won't even feel a thing." And with an instantaneous motion of his hand, a dark orb was formed and plunged into the electric mare's chest.

Max looked away before he could see the mare's lifeless body plunge to the ground. He held in a sob, ready to burst. His throat was achy and knotted. He was compelled to look, seeing Vexa's static die out like a candle being blown out by the wind.

But even as Vexa's static vanished, Melanie took in a renewed gasp of air. She was now breathing, and the color of her skinned returned to normal. She wriggled her fingers, reached her arms out into the air, and sat up, fully conscious. She stood up slowly, muscles taut from lack of use.

At first Melanie wondered where she was. She knew not, in the deep recesses of her mind, where she could possibly be. The room's ceiling towered high above, reaching impossibly far skyward. Then she turned her head a semicircle to look around. She saw a boy and two horses. *Max, Elzara, and Delveen*, she thought, excited. She ran to Max and the Nightmares. But if she had turned her head another half circle, she would have seen her own guardian, lying lifeless on the ground.

Max was hugged by Melanie, who then hugged the two Nightmares. He was happy that she was alive but also sad that Vexa was dead. Soon, Melanie would see.

"Where is Vexa?" she asked obliviously as she let go her embrace on Elzara.

There was a long pause. No one wanted to tell her what had just taken place.

"Why, she is over here," said the lead Shadowan, cackling like a hyena.

Silence fell for a moment but was then renewed.

"Who said that …" Melanie's sentence trailed off as she turned to see her protector on the ground. "Noooo!" she screamed as she darted to the still-warm corpse. She knelt by its side and wept hysterically. Tears flowed from her eyes like in a torrent.

Max was tense. He again held in a cry.

"And because I'm a … *creature* of my word, I will release the boy," the red-caped brute said, waving his hand. He signaled toward the Shadowan who Max and the Nightmares had chased here. That creature then placed both hands on the transparent ball, and with a quick gesture, the ball disintegrated. Justin was free, but obviously greatly weakened. He coughed and gasped for air.

Coming to his wits, Justin was about to run from the Shadowa when he was grabbed by the nape with a rough hand, nails piercing his neck. The sovereign Shadowan threw Justin to a nearby underling, who held the boy strongly by the arms.

"Give him to us!" Delveen cried, stomping forward. "This wasn't part of the deal, you hideous—"

The head Shadowan cackled once more and said, "Yes it was. I said I would release him, not return him to you. I thought you Nightmares were smart."

8

SUPERNOVA

You can't trust a Shadowan, Max pondered. The Crystal of Spei's three shards were still held by the superior Shadowan. It laughed, amazed by his own brilliance.

What are we going to do now? Max wondered anxiously. They were short one Nightmare, Justin was still captive, and Melanie was crying her eyes out. There were at least thirty demons in the room, not counting any that could be invisible.

"I knew there was something shady here," said Delveen. "This was all part of your plan. You convinced us into thinking that you were actually going to return Justin, but it was all a lie. Just a façade so you could keep the crystal and Justin."

"Good job," the sovereign creature chortled. "Didn't you like the plan? Wasn't it … *evil?*" It waited for a reply, but none came. "Well, I thought it was. Nevertheless, sucking the boy's soul is the next thing on our to-do list. And Nomed will succeed with pleasure."

A Shadowan from the left side of the leader, whose name must have been Nomed, strode forward, chuckling in a sinister way. He walked up to Justin, still detained by another Shadowan. He thrust his arms backward, collecting dark energy. His chest opened up slowly, beginning its process of removing the human soul that Max had seen up close once before.

The leader grabbed the weeping Melanie while the Nightmares and Max were looking at Nomed who charged up the dark orb. Max just watched. He could do nothing. In fact, he believed there was nothing they *could* do. Justin would die, and Melanie would too. In reality, Max would probably also. He had no hope. He was again as hopeless as when he'd first encountered Elzara in his room. How could he have hope when the Nightmares, the guardians with amazing strength and beauty, were able to be outsmarted by the evil, demon-like Shadowa?

Delveen's vines were poised, short for now but targeting each and every one of the Shadowa. Elzara saw the vines and contemplated what they could do to stop this from ending in tragedy. Then she knew that it was time.

Elzara looked at Delveen, who saw the fire horse's blazing eyes beaming with outstanding determination. She knew the look and quickly knew the plan. "Elzara, you can't. You may perish," the vine mare admonished softly, hoping there could be another way.

"Delveen," Elzara began lightly, "I must do this. It is the only way to stop them."

Delveen nodded. She understood what was at stake and that the predicament's only escape was for Elzara to do what she had to do, no matter how hard it would hurt in the end.

Max, a ways behind them, wondered what the Nightmares were talking about. Was it something involving him? Or was it something about the situation at hand? He became uneasy and anxious.

Nomed finished summoning energy. He was now ready to extract Justin's soul, when all of a sudden a blazing flame burst, blinding everyone in the vast room and warming everyone's face with radiance. Max looked at the brilliant blaze, squinting with difficulty. He couldn't see much besides the orange-red glow that shone like the sun. But just as quickly as it had formed, the light dimmed, leaving Max seeing green spots. He rubbed his eyes in attempt to clear the etchings in his vision, all the while hearing groans and screeches. He heard wings fluttering also. Then at last he was able to see where the groaning was coming from.

Elzara was entirely aflame, shooting fire orbs at each demon. Her fireballs spurted in rapid sequence like a machine gun, and her every shot was precise and meticulous. Her agility was perfect; she was now flying around at top speed, dodging dark balls here and there. She looked fearsome with her flames wound around her. The she stopped. Waves burst from her, like static from a live wire. She looked as though she was charging energy. After a few seconds, she let loose all the gathered power in a beam, blasting toward the tribe of Shadowa. The blast was like a nuclear bomb in sound and power. It was deadly and deafening.

Max's ears popped, and he found he couldn't hear anything. The blast pushed him to the ground. He scraped his elbows and felt a sharp pain in his tailbone as he fell. Within moments, his hearing came back, hearing nothing but fire cracking as he looked on. The tower-like room was filled with flames. The room glowed a luminous orange.

Max saw Melanie a short distance away, clutching her bleeding knuckles. Justin's pants were on fire until he noticed and patted them out in sheer panic. He looked as though he still couldn't hear, for he kept scanning the area, wide-eyed in panic. He mouthed words, but then cried as he realized his transient deafness.

Delveen swiftly galloped to Max and told him to gather the others. Then she dashed off to the heap of limp Shadowan bodies.

Max scrambled to his feet and gathered Melanie, then Justin, who now could hear once more. They ran to Delveen. Delveen was sniffling in what must be the Nightmare version of crying. And what she was crying for was Elzara, who laid wheezing and gasping for air on the floor. Max knelt by her side and wept as well.

Elzara struggled to move her lips and managed to say weakly, "Do not … weep, for this … is what … I was called—" She had a dreadful coughing fit, and then she continued, "—to do. I was not … meant … to see this … to the … end. Unite … the crystal … shards … and—" more coughing, "—you all … will become … Light …" She was unable to finish. Her line went flat.

They all broke out in tears, even Delveen. Max wept ferociously. He was furious also. *Why must this happen?* he pondered angrily.

Elzara was dead. Death swept through and took her, extinguished her life. She lay still, her heart no longer beating its regular *lub-dub*.

Delveen tried to stop crying. She finally managed to say, through the neighs and whimpers, to the three children who had come so far from their previous hopelessness, "She went supernova for the sake of you Dark Souls. She made the sacrifice. Now unite the fragments of the Crystal of Spei, and it will be finished."

They walked slowly to where the crystal shards had been. They found the lead Shadowan, now a corpse, holding the throbbing crystal shards with both hands. The Dark Souls took the crystal pieces and with hope united them together. White light shone brightly from the newly intact crystal.

9

A HOPEFUL HEART

Max began to float off the ground. A good ten inches into the air, his left slipper fell off. Frigidness wrapped itself around Max's foot, sending a chill upward through his body. He looked down slightly. Melanie and Justin weren't rising. Why? Weren't they making the transition from Dark Soul to Light Soul?

"Bye, Max," Melanie said. "Stay hopeful."

Justin looked at Max and added, "Don't doubt."

"Well done, Max Weston. You are now a Light Soul." Delveen's voice was strong despite her recent crying.

Max felt a rush of glee race through his bloodstream. He was happy and blissful. And then the magnificent white light shone to such a full brightness that Max could not see.

Max lay in his bed. He looked around—no Delveen, Melanie, or Justin. No flames, no radiance. Just the darkness of night. He threw the covers off himself and went to put on his slippers. Only one was present. He pondered for a brief moment before remembering that he lost the other in the towering room.

He walked out his room, down the hallway, and silently slipped into his parents' room. He shook his mother. She stirred and then fully awoke. "What are you doing up at—" she paused to look at the alarm clock on her night table and continued "—at five in the morning?"

"It's five in the morning? But it was nearly daytime when I was in the tall room," Max said, ignoring his mom's inquiry, speaking mostly to himself.

"A tall room? What?" Mrs. Weston asked.

"Nothing," Max said. "Probably a dream. Good night." Max frowned, and then smiled.

"Good night, Max," his mother said, yawning.

Max softly treaded down the hall to his room, thinking. *How could it have been a dream? It felt so real. It was so detailed. I felt pain.* He was slightly confused, but soon he began to see things clearly. He sat on his bed with a joyful expression pasted on his face. At least, he knew, he had completed the journey that he must. He was now living with a faithful heart. He hoped that everything would be fine and knew now to never doubt, for the journey he had traversed had involved much faith in the Crystal of Spei changing him.

It was all a dream. But he had completed his journey toward living life. Living life with a hopeful heart, hoping in goodness. Mankind was not doomed after all.

Max looked around his room and saw shadows from the trees outside his window. *There will be darkness clouding over you, stalking you like a shadow.* Max looked down at the toys on the floor. A stallion action figure lay beside the deck of cards he'd spilled before and his math textbook. How did that get there?

You'll always have a guardian—loving you, teaching you, showing you the way to truth. Max smiled as he thought of Elzara, his equestrian guide.

He looked up at the wall and saw a singed area near the closet door. He turned over to see the chestnut frame holding a picture of his friends Craig, Leah, and Kris. He was sad, but he recalled the good times they had had. The smiles on their faces showed it. Live life to the fullest. Love your family and friends. They are there to help smooth out life's bumpy ride.

Max's brother's bright nightlight's illumination sneaked its way from the hall into Max's room. It formed a gentle, triangular glow that reminded Max of the Crystal of Spei he had gathered in the Shadowa stronghold, way up in the mesosphere. He pondered its luminescence—black, crimson, and white. He was sure of the meaning now. And he smiled. He closed his eyes. He sighed a sigh of relief and was filled with hope—hope everlasting. He also thought about darkness and light. Even in the dark you can still see the light. Light will endure evermore.

Max reclined in his bed, pulling the wool quilts over his body for warmth, for it was certainly below thirty degrees.

THE END

www.ingramcontent.com/pod-product-compliance
Lightning Source LLC
Chambersburg PA
CBHW022052170626
46808CB00003B/1450